10.95
'EW

INTO DISTANCES

Other Books by Aaron Shurin

Woman on Fire
The Night Sun
Toot Suite
Giving up the Ghost
The Graces
Elsewhere
A's Dream
Narrativity

INTO DISTANCES

AARON SHURIN

Sun & Moon Press
LOS ANGELES

Sun & Moon Press
A Program of The Contemporary Arts Educational Project, Inc.
a nonprofit corporation
6026 Wilshire Boulevard, Los Angeles, California 90036

First published in paperback in 1993 by Sun & Moon Press
10 9 8 7 6 5 4 3 2 1
FIRST EDITION

This book was made possible, in part, through grants from the California Arts Council, the National Endowment for the Arts, and through contributions to The Contemporary Arts Educational Project, Inc., a nonprofit corporation

Some of these poems previously appeared in *The Archive Newsletter*, *Avec*, *Central Park*, *Conjunctions*, *Dark Ages Clasp the Daisy Root*, *Five Fingers Review*, *Grand Street*, *New American Writing*, *Notus*, *Poetics Journal*, *Raddle Moon*, *ReMap*, *Screens and Tasted Parallels*, *Sulfur*, *Temblor*, and *ZYZZYVA*. The author thanks the editors of these publications.

Cover: *Westward Ho* by Edward Ruscha, 1986
Dry pigment and acrylic on paper, 60 1/8" x 40 1/4"
reproduced by permission of the artist
Design: Katie Messborn

LIBRARY OF CONGRESS CATALOGING IN PUBLICATION DATA
Shurin, Aaron (1947)
Into Distances
p. cm — (New American Poetry Series: 13)
ISBN: 1-557131-122-8
I. Title. II. Series.
811'.54—dc19
CIP
Printed in the United States of America on acid-free paper.

CONTENTS

INTO DISTANCES

BREATH

Wandering air, white teeth over his lips, alone in the house went over to the bed — her window folded away in his brain. A dark apple; evening reddened at the edges. He sighed, sat down to pour the tea. In the same tone, one imagines it didn't exist.

He put a hoof to the doorway, come out. The wind freshened his mouth, his eyes quivering. Tonight, in the dark, he wants that wavering path. Tonight the slow growth of heresies in his eyes, vigilant, disarming, fleeing. Into the hands of the winds in shirtsleeves, scramble him out again. He dried the page without listening, their voices bleaching the air.

Pointing his finger: the same room: empty. You must feel the black sheet, the blue error. Beat the air these years his eyes are wanderers. He came forward again and set them free.

He came following through a body, watch it flow past. A quiver through the slits, walking wearily. He breathes upward, anywhere, homing, swallowing hard. The night fades around his milky veil. . . .

A UNION

You are my aim, my impatience, my anger, my morning in a little country; go away, please!

He went out, the swirl of the smell of her small feet, thatched armpit; under the gate he waited, she was crouching in fear. He recognized his poetic paradise.

These conversations would answer "Yes, I remember!" The tops of the trees rising in front of them when the musty furniture gave in, she clipped and kept her distance, rolling him like a ball of bread, he would seize the shape of her fingers, whirl about in these luminous bars. Certain clouds are made to be breathed in.

He glued his lips to an air of resignation. At the same time she puts on her dragon's helmet. I'm a fool and exhibit myself for money. His hands were burning and every minute passed.

Why should a being be couched in a load of particulars? Now and then with head thrown back and mouth wide open. Whole body growing thinner, he threw his desperate arms around her neck, "My precious doll!" She even tried to sing an absolute lullaby; he shivered along the length of the whole song. Hours counted the minutes; probably a sacrifice was being made. The rain fell out there on the pavement, pushing insolence to the limit.

It's tomorrow, everything is ready, your promise is ripe. You are my repetition, my distance, my here and there, my dark background. Slowly their silence obtained a more delicious lie. The device laid bare their incorporeality; he squeezed her hand to encourage that sort of thing.

The houses are swarming — rumblings and cracklings lick the silk. They embrace in a blackening orange light, their sensibility responds to its caress. The sun or the rain entered the house, imitation lace; reverently an air of repose curtained the whole room. They are shadows in a window, saving each other in private. A smell of wet leaves envelops their loss.

HIS PROMISE

Yesterday, I have always seen him. I followed him into Paris: here was the entrance. In the light — and hearing — luxury descended over soothing waves, the boulevard with the sign of fraternal beatitude.

If I give their eyes then I have never seen eyes. Seated, we ate/drank the hours. Impalpable useless smoked slowly soul, and familiarity shown, say, in a homesick pact. I lifted my glass and of its creation: perfectibility! His aroma explained progress up to the present moment.

I share a reputation admitted beloved brothers, possession in every corner persuade the devil his brimming pleasures. On this subject I've met with the most invisible companions. We bow to each other like memory, to wipe out old grudges.

At last, shivering, sung by poets and philosophers, it said to me, "I want to take you away." Famous remembrance, "to compensate for your loss I shall come seeking you." Flattery and adoration know all this intoxication, flowers warm as he rose me with a smile. . . .

To thank him I left him, little by little crept back to bed. On my knees at the feet of that vast assembly I murmured my prayers: his promise. Half asleep with indifference I seemed to remember waiting for him before. . . .

He unlocked one hand, her legs pointed softly in the chair. She surged and felt the pulse on his face, plunged a hand in. Open to the light the purple window busted blood. This dump with a private balcony and his black moustache.

"I'll miss you too" and across the room he punched out another breath. Under the smells his sweet trumpet to a whisper down his back. From niceness there still crawled a blond's voice.

She scissored and a blue rose above the dress was limp at best. There was the gaping bed over her again — touched things he had touched — her boneless exhaustion carrying the room. His left leg shook inside his trousers.

There was no dance floor. Her milky eyes laughed and his hair came up. They stayed very small, leaned against the wall for years, a cloudless sky there was nothing in but both of them.

They were loose, they were dark, they seeped into the night, shade of wound, scorched on the casual floor, undressed my brains, the roots of her hair grow in the bedroom, his opening other room across himself, she was out there.

Watch this: he put a finger to the same spot — the same finger — and let fall a moon whiter than his twisted knuckles. He wiped his face to the door, glanced back, and listened. Soundlessly a carpet of uncanny brightness.

THE THIRD FLOOR

John said, "Hit me again," looked down at his own hand. He held his mouth close to him with a cool greenish flicker. The instrument pulled, sipped it slow, he said "Are we a couple of guys?" He jammed a thick one into his whole face.

"Huh?" Dave lowered his eyebrows — frail body come apart in wisps — muscles leaned around him through a maze of rubbed fire, bony fingers. He dusted and waited, looked tired, reached across the table purringly licked his lips. With a thick finger he said "Yeah."

The frontal bones stood up. His right hand twisting in the air, polished from sunlight, brown and slender and poised. A tearing sound dragged across his tongue and teeth.

John turned, holding his hand against the sandy skin of his face. "Take it." With a sidelong look thick sobs and hard eyes like a safe. He formed a wadded mass, flared, almost nodded — there was a long wait, a whirring of leaves against the glass, a husky voice got him at last. "Don't take it too big."

Something was empty in his deep eyes. An open cut between needles that ran into his palm. There wasn't any back door on a chopping block.

Dave bent down and touched the sticky place shocked and stiff. His whipped-out nerves shivered, started up somewhere, swelled in sound and faded. "Yeah," he said softly, foamy against the corner. He got in and coasted.

John spoke in a tight snapped voice. Down a narrow corridor to a big window stabbing the sky. His face in the dark undressed to the skin. He sipped that, throaty, was blurred.

Dave turned slowly, looked down at him. His white eyes knotted and jerked his head at an inner door.

"You're my partner."

INTO DISTANCES

I.

The sky: the sea with wings. There have been days I would stand gazing for hours in diversity. From these fragments, from causes, power, poverty, I belong to experience.

She labored down the path barefoot, the wind wrapped her body, shadowed by clustering blossoms and velvety sunshine. I remember her unhappy married life as more children arrived, taking hold of me on all sides in one spot of my will — "stomp me into the ground." I lied, she was never close to the wind. The fat flowers laughed. I was hardened and have no meaning.

We looked: sweeping down the approaching road it grew louder, rushed against the flat earth roaring. Smell and hear and see and feel everything! I listened to the voice and knew it sucked up all the air around us. Slowly I was learning shame and secrecy, forced joy behind the hen-house, slept off something wrong, shook me nameless and struck my body with perfection and disgust. His word was enough for me, though I knew he'd never be his word.

My grandmother when there is no moon. She possessed all and assumed control, milked the cows with the movements of a man, skimmed under her hands the dawn and carried pistons to bed at night. In private no man could look her in the eye; her thick hair would appear in the door: she walked immune. At my tears she would use it on me: "You're unornamented, girl!" That was long ago; I walk hand in hand with unloveliness that gave distinction to destruction. Anyone elaborated the story through my silence.

While the cold sky came driving down to the grass with dew, the men cut firewood, the women peeled and sliced. If you looked at them you felt as if you'd worked yourself, who pass greeting over the hills, family honor under the cedar trees, torture their wives, show no resentment, work again, hard filled with labor our house smooth as night.

Now around through the crowd on the platform music. His silver buckle distinguished him, he knew all the songs, he was young and called for the dance. Everyone bowed, separated, flaming light in the center they met, flying around and drifting clouds. His side, her face, her hands, his bending shoulder. I climbed before me a sea of swinging figures, rushed me under the raised legs and skirts. And the calling! . . . all the good things . . . listening . . . I was so little!

The slaughtering smoking winter filled mounds. You threw in a handful of corn and you could eat into deep plates. Was my name Standing Farther, Cooler and

Tougher, Virgin Whiteness, Bleeding Arrows? Was there a secret tale in my voice that continued at midnight when the stars were creeping, quarreling into my child life money terror, dog work, disobey, placed my hand where we were not; tears fell on it.

We went by covered wagon, reached a forest, and stopped. Under the sky I stood on the yielding earth, her eyes were black, transitoriness came and swept the hills into distances. She stood facing north and west and south. I must turn around again and carry down words. It has been years with ease and swiftness. They came soundlessly over the wheel of the sky.

If you want to run away don't tell stories. She turned swiftly and gazed at her standing there. She could not hide the eyes still young and flared open. I began to make up a story — that eventuality between me and the door — pushed by the sky and some wind carrying me on its back. I would say I was walking down the road and slipped into smooth clouds, long time. We all stood and melted together, there where that black speck was gone. . . .

II.

The town was occupied — Strike! — bullets flying on our side of the river. The law restored the convicted back in the ground. In the dark tunnels long hours dug and dragged it to the end of the month. I passed in a foreign tongue, ceaselessly preparing for another construction.

She kept her eyes on the edge of an excavation. I have seen that look in other eyes, in love with a terrible thing and submerged in another: I can show each night. The men mixed with clay — foul-mouthed and trusting — spent it in one night. She befriended the men, alone in the darkness humble before infinity. The lean one was one of these; the men exchanged glances; big to her and gleamed with smothered laughter. He called to me and I slipped in. We passed through a canyon, and you can have this horse I'm riding.

If you open a book you have to write in it. I fled beyond the bitter tracks we had made. The gleaming road leapt forward like water, moonlight ice with prairie grass and purple hills. Animals cried there, and stretched on stones. Beyond them mountains called the snows into crevices.

You passed empty houses — The Flats — coyotes left their hiding places. The saloon, the schoolhouse, the Company. Miners — boys! — eating and breeding; the next strike; hunger would not give credit. I heard the possessors deserve the world of knowledge. There was silence about her for miles, I remade her silence. She would turn without a word, would gather the hills, would follow the same tune unrolling in the wind. Once, I myself knew it, in one spot on the hard, packed earth.

She worked and buried her head at night, knew little of theory but turned loose her convictions upon them. Could she tear the petrified trees from the earth by their roots? It beat rhythmically, climbed the flight of stairs, the end of "education" and enemy of women, began to draw the veil of forgetfulness down over desire. I was my wind as I sit here with leaves about me. I wrote down my name in actions not suitable for position.

If they told a story I understood their purpose. Grave things drawn beyond their depths. As I wrote I recalled — a laborer can turn her hand — pushed upward, staring at it, connected, convicted. Words are nothing but words — then gradually they were streets. I walked, there were trees flowing, earth against my body, face down in work and sleep. And those up there: his mouth and eyes, my mother with mud, the company store. She had come before me, a woman and a stranger, muscular arms and wilderness under the skin. The word subjects her to the circle to be pure and repeated. Words cannot erase experience.

The train was an entreaty, but did not buy a ticket to leave. I marched and searched their faces. The lines — their falling music — would not be ended. . . .

III.

At night the wind from the mesa could reach and I rode safely. Mingling with wailing to demonstrate "learned something." Yes, they are a part of her blood, forming far from town the cold lightning across my doorway. I erased those dead songs from my tongue.

Springtime, up the fuzzy hills, the river higher, rushing each night in our ears. In the semi-darkness the shouting between us was already filled. I cried out, waded under, crept nearer, clung to mine. Lights were burning like an animal that has eaten. The swaying water sailing away, hung in the willow trees, sated; in the morning the world is gone. Today is shivering, those were my blood and bodies, far back from the dark mountains in the flood.

Listen and look intelligent — you have grammar and a few more things, cook their food, wash bed, made skirts in her big-veined hands — a short distance from the rock rim for hours. Names and addresses contained patterns; from this short list I chose these working shoulders.

Ah! — house! — drive me over the hills tomorrow! One day my mother was sick and I must go home. Up the canyon road the scrub oak pulling at the frozen ground — only thinking, feeling nothing — separate units exhausted distances, down the lashing road must be coaxed a faltering child. I stumbled the steps, beyond the windows shattered into bits . . . three days and nights would awaken me . . . tiny eyes in the next room . . . clasped her unfamiliar hand . . . I would not give it nourishment. That morning was there. In my arms she tore back her yearning and pulled me to my feet. Speech contracted in circles, and I understand nothing except this thing.

Turning away her face from us stood watching that kicking baby. We began in a station and met swept clean across the plains. She followed her silence in every direction, calling down the wind and the rain accusingly. Her eyes swooped upon its prey: I did not weep.

She grew stronger, tightly about me, my body between them. Tangled in the folds and had laughed herself into solemnity. To me her living the same way made theirs — more rights over body and soul — pledged by such things to self-respect and conviction. We would go there — my voice continued — into a world.

A woman arrived in town with palm trees on the shores. The network of light — of tracks — regarded her with surprise. "Is there a train due here?" "You're too early," and vanished from her face. Hunger wondered if she could stand on her feet; every word uttered about her sought its way to food. She went away ethereal and almost pleasant. The wind in the tree far back recorded the floor.

Now long afterward my legs trembled when I stood. We talked of that intellectual world where waves of thought sweep for the depths, of work and nearly starved, of resentment downstairs, traveled farther, weeping women, the eastern sky passing the dawn through material things. In a canyon, flowing by my bones, the river cooled.

The trail had guarded these rugged hills, black, stony, frying. Her head touched the ground in greeting, where the trees began to grow again. Into an arroyo and came up on the other side. At dusk the giant cacti, arms against the sky. Where the wind haunting the mountain captured her penetrated friendship. In the center, the string around, she was crossing over, changing places; the peculiar fierce movements of her body beneath me tore through the air. Neck to neck, the wind sweeping her hair back, lathering, rearing and whirling; through her muscles and her lips I received the quivering water.

IV.

Slowly the train came toward me, I heard her teasing voice. My face, my eyes, my skin and hair, moved forward. "I made them," then I turned and watched her. Voices here and there, heavy sleep, across the darkness we lay there, "this life couldn't stand you," or "I couldn't stand this life." I used to be strong . . . going to get work . . . died away uncovered and lay staring through the window. The watching stars seemed good or bad. Far up in a slumber a figure endured experience.

They told me what they believed, now you tell me who did that. The rich are interested in prostitution; let any man judge my nobody body. In my work her head blossoms and bent, a woman actively doing something. Dark and silent were the mansions who live and sleep in peace and luxury — they dug him out and his mouth was filled with mud. Belief and reason went again to the circle.

Little dried-up dances could reply to such arguments. I have learned and become a force, and the tea in my cup became cold. Before the sun comes up invaders mingled their customs. Their fragrance came to me with the shadow of purple skies, and the slender forefinger traveling across the page. I shall remember the past, perhaps the present, but the future dissected everything.

It has no fear, no money. Our heads were spreading, a touch of wistfulness in it. It comes back, as if I were a part of the air. Talk to me, I was a raw, impulsive woman, and work was intense. Let affection make conviction the basis of your action. I am organizing and fighting for the wind.

SAILED

Under a sky, in a garden, there are serious women and beautiful men, were talking. "You are much more beautiful," they implore, and can't help their red cheeks from flaming. "You are terrifying, too," and speak in the same voice.

He is already far away, is going to other trees on the horizon, disappear behind that cloud and drew around him closer a sleeping voice, lowered to a rolling feeling. In the dark she is sleeping, stroking on forever, buried in her hair this garden while the eyes of stupefaction widened, and the light curls lighting up this boy in the clouds would find him in some thick aureole covering her back and waking somewhere else. . . .

I walk straight ahead, pays attention without always seeing, playing music the way I'd like to live. His lamentations would bring the cymbals together. I wanted to find out where they were enjoying themselves, followed them at a distance to where the beautiful nights dance like bears. I've remembered a cup of brandy, and went to sleep turned toward their faces, the stars.

From the air there was his eye in his forehead, the sun had a brother. One of them said, "Yesterday moves so slowly." One of them said, "Seemed to linger with pleasure in the great hollow sky." One of them said, "Each setting out in solemnity from a beautiful night like this. . . ."

They give what she has, and wind up here for the future. How many refugees between birth and death, wrapped in white paper as its name works, she inserts between teeth. The hard peach, the sour gray bread, the small pears in their skin.

In the evening we stroll off the long day, setting across her bed. Air by the river beaten down with the heat; spotless blue keeps her troubles neatly within. The children in their eye, wide mouth, cascade ear; the hillsides — poplars — with the shadows and hues of tapestries. Everyone is singing the praises of goose fat and bacon.

Where I was born in a grocer's cellar made me think of women wide at the hip. Over there his sleepy eyes this way of blue, eyelashes going wisp of smoke, to the fields with melting sugar as he folds his lips . . . fresh, penetrating pine . . . his path with dangling arms, furry under dew, murmuring up against pebbles into the rhythm of water and dry leaves.

Meaning and sonority descend the slope. The golden weight of attention. His two hands altered the sound of his voice, swooping the air one clenches. The wind can snap them up this exhalation.

We lie on the grass in the grass, our ears spread passage. Covers us and ignores us, thinned with sunlight and heat.

Pass between the leaves enunciated sky, between our whirlwind heads, shutterless. Under the swallows, turning empty air. . . .

TEMPTATION

The stairs of sleeping climbed against the first night with real gods. Communicates with him an imperious air of ambiguous sex. And of his body softness, heavy eyes, vague lips, lifted its head and suspended vials of personages in relief. He sighed, secret insects of his breath hung in the illuminated air, warm, purple, and turned toward him with shining eyes.

His hand spread the contagion of a golden chain — look down as he was, attracting to yourself the sculptor of clay. In a melodious voice of insidious pleasure escaping a greater master.

If you wish, keep your remembering; the second air insinuating vast proportions hung down over his thigh. His hurrying skin representing figures to lose themselves in yours. Recognize that perfumed beauty in another being, you forget your dubious disadvantages.

This one said "procure everything!" Seems to hold their fascination as of voice — huskiness washed with echo — and the seductive trumpet of those pipes reverberated the unbridled air.

A laugh went rolling, bore the indecent names. A certain person drinking his fury somewhere. Still musky with pleasure he lifted his eyes, looking for actual men. In truth I am awake, begging them to forgive me.

CONTINUOUS THUNDER

There exist rebels, strange possession joined a conspiracy and in question were arrested. Worthy men consult death — his favorite player — he was a lover of morals — the fine arts of enemy have won him a historian. Write anything for pleasure, one forms a vast stage for his monster forms.

Suddenly one of his most famous roles probed deeper: "condemned to die." When people are using an expression they can still distinguish the actor, the day arrived. He walked and saw a singular beauty in the impersonation of the possible real. To me, believing in the idealization as alive, a fury blended my eyes for you around his head that irrefutable way, trembles has never left me, beams invisible while I look for words but visible to me. And that abyss, on the edge of paradise, does not see the whole audience.

Everyone gave himself up to the voluptuous pleasures of the grave. The noise joined him without a qualm of mourning. Did he feel in his forecasts the striking justifications flouted in his face as I watched the pallor compressed and applauded his fire? At a certain moment his lips flashed across his face, he left.

A few minutes later a hiss awakened; the theater of his mouth fell backward. There is ground for the last time —

sweet and large — but none has been able to rise. They say he was almost one of the friends, a discontented attraction; those like myself staggered forward a step. No punishment remained.

THE DEPOSITORIES

The enemy personified the nation. A fiction or series of fictions exploding through with smoke, pouring sweat. At the foot of a tree hands stuck in the dirt. Once in a while they hold on to me.

A couple of them seemed to be moving around the field, black-eyed, loose splinters from the neighborhood, full of wasted determination. He coughed it up on the pillow in a sort of puddle. The forms lying there, vacant, removed from there.

The house thin, blue, hanging in the air, transparent in the trees, the forms of the trees, no partition whichever way you move. . . .

This man was weak, received a box from home, munching on a bloody cracker in the remaining hand. Two boatloads arriving, exposed to it anywhere, torches on the ground, rags around heads, hot at night with sudden energy, the maintaining skin of vengeance. Green oozing out from the grass — large spaces swept over — burning the dead beards, odor of the rejected arm and leg. In history the paper remain and still remain, soaking up the glaze. . . .

I sit by his shining hair, the heart of the stranger. His ashy eyes, roasted in the morning. As you pass by, be on guard where you look. Opposite my window the freed horses are led off. The smoke streams upward, dark, thick, warm.

He said, "Make your own choice." The kiss I gave him discharged better views.

The man is struggling for breath; a soldier's life must be a bent thing. Others are arranged in a straight row. They have some old magazines I was in the habit of reading: theory, practice, democratic premises, superfluity. He was an ideal of his age in a few days. He kept a diary and wrote, "The doctors have been brave."

I am taking care of a silent rebel, laid down on his arm to see its distribution, lying on the spot that time a hole in the air, his small calculations extruded. Meat might be named from mere demonism; nature and pretense were there.

I like to stand and look a long while. Individuals in human places verify the forms. The dim leaden members with heads leaning and voices speaking. In the arms and in the legs from my observation.

Dear Madame, I have seized the testimony, still alive. I do not know his past life, but feel as if it must have been good. I saw circumstances, and can give you some fragmentary physiognomy and idioms. . . .

Flesh of his breast and tremulous arms in the strain of a partial sleep, I have a special friend. Out of the shadowy scene the white beds, sat by a huddled form, shone in through the window a vacant moon. . . .

Buttons . . . tufts of hair . . .
In bushes, low gullies, or on the sides of hills. . . .

CONSTRUCTOR

In the morning it is still night; what you lose shakes off his dawn with difficulty. It opens nocturnally wide, casts its nets, takes hold of children, rolled up like turbans, encircles the feet, the quivering petals grow bigger. For such voluminous pressure on the poor rugged women I have been asked to extend regulation, the slowed down economy of thick obscure writing.

Do not wake up. Let yourself half open. Relaxed, follow the handle which divides into two legs; crack your lightened body and cross the silences for confidences. Trust the ambiguous hour of my window to gossip. They serve you chocolate which loosens tongues, vapor lower down, berated, "Ssh!", undertone, tonic, mouth to ear. And that presence of a trembling creature who struggles to keep quiet about false love. "Come in, and seek some information."

From her room a woman descends in many other houses. Imperative, though it disguises itself as the outer shadow. Personal surface climbs or descends the glacial staircase, pursuing a kitchen studded with copper and yarn. It brought company to begin with, the small events of a time.

It depicts what it has seen. It is well on the way to connecting those little tools with black handles. Beneath the conversation, pierced and repierced with openings. . . .

AN EXHIBITION

Bearded men, somewhere in the vicinity of sepulchers. The oaken door seemed never to have known the street. On one side a black rose rooted in the civilized soil, kept alive on the threshold of narrative to determine some inauspicious darkening. It might be a sluggish child, scourged and driven into the shadow of discipline and law. Morally as well as materially the women stood within a century.

From within the door there appeared a gray woman, the sunshine threw off a face of regularity, black eyes, startled and shone out misfortune, recklessness, desperate peculiarity, enclosing her female spectators. She has felt the grim gesture stitched to her shoulders. Open a passage! This time extremity is dragged into the sunshine!

She was there for them to spurn, know the intensity of a historical machine, in the grasp of the public head, she ascended this engine on proneness, flagrant gripe, displayed above the street: her part. And the image of this shuddering smile made the world darker for beauty.

They would find a theme in an exhibition like the present. It must have been the presence of men looking down from the platform, risking majesty. Herself the object, each man each woman their individual parts. When the whole scene seemed to vanish she was the most conspicuous object before them, intermingled with recollections. Another moment half-obliterated by point of view.

One came swarming back upon her stricken beauty, eyes bleared had a purpose — worn materials in these shifting scenes — came back feeding all the assembled regards. It sent a cry to assure herself that these were her realities, and the public had awaited her. From this consciousness of observation a convulsive force was pressed.

Old volumes and old portraits have to step forth. Compressed upon her face fixed arms, a whole people, burning down her face and lighting up a voice behind her. "I've been privileged to sit in the presence of so great a multitude." She bent her eyes to look inward. The interior air remained entire.

CONNECTION

The morning of her bed, of her girlhood, lived next to the telephone; slid open to reveal her body talking to a sexy boy. Modern girls don't have to wait before a shop window. Our hero, standing on end, took a step: it felt so good.

His voice across her bedsheets, licking from inside under her eyes, his fingers went to pieces, sunlight mounted memory and steamed down the vertical slot. She heard a voice: "I'm here. Hold on."

What was she thinking of? I go where I'm interested — then I'm not a woman. Bloated with light and air, she looked up to see her mother standing in the doorway. A dull monologue on how she really feels deep down.

Her optimism sloshes in circles, her thirst for something grand slipping further and closer. She stands and lifts arms, shallow breathing because a phone's ringing; I want to be there in the mechanism, to leave a message on the moth-eaten rug. I wore a long white undershirt — never again anything purer — watching the night with its moving hands as they touched my thighs, my hips charged with symmetry. Tick away around in circles, shimmying the air. . . .

The city floated in her uneven breathing, pushing from beneath the ladder to the sheets and spreads between us, just the morning. A girl leaned into the phone: distance was speaking. From the crown of her head a wave down her spine brought it all back. Her totemic privacy was mine to give away. The window bursts pink, staining the pillowcase.

ONE EVENING

They're ready. The three of them with that. One starts, then falls into arms. Lines into flowing gowns where the low-ceilinged truth governs.

We're dancing — distort sufficiently — for the pleasure of identities overlap, and their faces remain secret against the ladies. The dress likes the way he looks, hairy; bends down, turn around, suggesting velvet cellos concealed by black silk. Down the stairs, young of the smoke, he would hide his moist eyes.

He takes him by the shoulders and thighs, throwing stones at the children for a sigh. Around the room masks are dancing downstairs. It was she who opened the door, pretending to fasten a garter, and the dawn went straight down to the sea.

At the top of the street his face was laughing, holding him by the arm; the audience was himself — his complement — his fancy dress and his imaginary nights. I would have taken his place; only the great know how to walk swaying, purging distance from the sky. He sang the roses to freshen them up, and every gesture opened the morning street to her windows and what goes on beneath them.

The air fluttered from top to bottom. Not a practical inventory. They heard bicycles, cleaning women, continued to sing on their secret road, cleared with perfume and suspended in sleep. They left behind make-believe gestures to make up her true nature. To think with precision she thought to herself, "I'm presence."

She was, through her submission, the idea of solidity. Her name was Broiling-Days-In-A-Little-Patch-Of-Shade. They made their way there, heavy with one summer evening; visiting the earth with powder and peopling it with kisses.

INSCRIPTION

Dear:

Tell me what the first name is. I've seen pictures, but the title you gave me isn't the one I meant. I suppose I wonder if you understand such a book — that landscape with its clay sky and still purer roofs. Every evening looks early in the morning, springing up into our whole body of light. His wings father other people in the things of everyday life.

We took a walk through corn fields as tall as a house, gray branches and black bushes of stones, the wind from the little white path blooming the wallflowers, and below the horizon projecting far into the sea. On the roofs of the houses I thought of you, not because I deserve it but because years cover all things. Goodbye to their parents which the boys wave from the window.

I would also like you to see the dark stairs with the rotten floor, and spend a winter with them in the past an oil stain on the your drawing. A little word is sometimes how you are.

When I think of the past, or rather my evil self, and the virtuous eyes of so many other treasure ships, or rather photographs, I bring forth out of their treasure things these things, or rather the room shedding itself . . .

If I

could work and not come back from where one has a view over the whole city, turnips, vines, roads, horses, drivers, I can follow the impossible lessons at a convenient distance and come out renewed. The path becomes a picture little by little; passers-by see only a bit of smoke. Those trees you see protect you, and the memories gather all under that one name.

I said to myself, "Shall I be here?", but he says to me, "You'll recover." So I left him a few masterpieces, and he said, "I've already seen too many inconveniences."

I have already written like strawberries in spring. With my realism secrets initiate me into the palette. Afterwards, the brains with the hands chose the active part of this homesickness.

Write to me soon without my always being conscious of it. Don't forget I like thick paper that wakes me up in the night. It's in the air — something that can't stand the light. I sent you a drawing of the open air — my hands just can't keep from working!

This is my ambition of such and such a person it is not the language of nature. You'll see from the outline the composition is shifting. Such a position can go forward or back through some opening, look through it, it is absolutely the thing — aside from a few other things.

I would give you the impression we saw leaves in the wood, shadows blotted streaks in the glow by the trees. From the ground those black stems wandering around the dark masses, that dark ground of red, yellow, white. The trunks were clotted and rooted in the light because it is impossible. Something has spoken to me that cannot be deciphered. The bushes are standing there.

Yours,

BLUE SHADE

She leaned in a small fist on the cushions, buds in her pajamas. "Make me a story about a tower room and fresh air."

There was a girl fluttering her fingers. She sent down for her peach-colored suitcase, the high clouds of the balconies. A whisper smiled his smile, smoothing the long waves of her name.

The hand of her opened slowly, hummed down and swelled a waltz over the carpet. A lazy push opened the door and started to slip in; the girl watched the shadow sprayed on the wall.

She's been here for days, wordless and plump. It went slowly. Syllables flicked at it and went away.

THE INTIMATE

I got him to tell me about M. Introduce me to M. He had told me in confidence that she was this:

On the first floor a perfect voice, wide-open. She had a sponge-like mass on the forehead, and a cleft in her nose. "I was splitting at every fold," she said, chatted together. I forced myself not to look at the wallpaper.

"Like most young things," she said, "I knew how to withdraw from people, return to them, then leave again. I was able to come and go without stirring from my chair." M's skin with red patches was ravished by her smile. The shape of her head was not ashamed of being novel.

As we sat under the fine needles I gave her advice concerning the edge of her eyelids; I made a little fringe high up on her cheekbones, near her temples. I promptly did not know what to do with her neck. "I have come to the end of my person," she said, "confined to a rare smoothness."

Friendship is particularly true when friendship is beginning. "If I were you I would do my hair like this."

IN

It was waiting for me, the streets, beers, and basement corridors. The women dressed up hot pictures good in that dress walked me into my breasts, we were smelling like strong arms when the music stopped. Her feet standing over me were falling into my shaking hands.

She stepped out of her dress; I slipped off my wig; she took off her earrings; I put on that nice girl. I could tell from her face I was happy.

Nostalgia might have a dress-up fetish; just thinking about it was everything white. Sky full of streetlight make you feel snow, pizza, polished nails, believe in affairs who they are with those cherry all over the floor.

Some people have coffee pots or a couple of magazines. Her story was made for illusion in expensive leather jackets — each name those pages on a marquee — girls hanging out with girls opened my mouth: a reflection came out. A real person was talking to me with blonde tips.

"Where are we going?"
"I have the key."
"People can go anywhere."
"They're different."
"I'm gonna be one too."
"They know where they live," she said; I handed her my sweets and shivered.
"You know the difference."

She went into the next room, her breasts in the next song. Her eyes on the open floor — what you want from me. Old lipstick lurked everywhere, thick and shiny and clutching that little piece of metal. The mouth myself — color what hurts most — I would kiss her ass lying face up looking for a little girl.

I remembered any time I chose, running my forefinger along its farther chamber. In and out of costumes — something very personal — riding the motorcycle highway with summer streaming behind you, put on my silky body billowing touchable, cowboy suede and played the jukebox, a private conversation and when it was over I was thrilled in the shadows.

She reached out with long hands and gave the woman a shove. Please let me stay, faster and faster, where earlier she was nowhere to be found. I watched how I reacted. She smelled like breathing — muscles tell how they really feel — on my neck to see her teeth changing my life.

She put her arms around me — big hands comes home at night — I think needing loving from her woman. She was so close in the lightest way waves of dark smoke. I breathed and stepped into the possibilities.

There is not a tree around; on the other hand there's an open invitation. The bird is not yet extinct as he flies his sorrows to sour peaches too far to walk.

We went slowly in the small air, a humming here and there; he spoke passing his hand over his thin eyes, and he looked at me without a trace of character. His attitude was one of supervision on the threshold of the half-open door. I admired his face of the evening sky — invades the warm body and closes the eyes, glow in the motionless hay, spring water, taking away. . . .

Next day I paid a call on old-man broad shouldered himself. The same little eyes engaged me in conversation. When he did so, I was conscious of a feeling that I was not really right. Below his breath I asked him, "Sir, shall I spend the night here in your shed?"

"You'll be welcome!" he shouted, I threw myself down on the sweet-smelling sheet. Behind him his sons came in one after the other. I was absorbed by my new acquaintances, their confidences, and lived from mouth to mouth; his protection was endowed with advantages to cure frenzy or bleeding, had the touch, and makes his way instinctively creep out to meet him. The bird after which he is named is completed.

"Is it the same way there?" I would exclaim. "Tell us, sir, how is it?" I can't tell you all the questions, but he doesn't mind undergoing the future, as if it had been carved out of mammoth skin. He would accompany himself on the balalaika, shut his eyes in the grass smells and sing: "We drove off, the sunset was just beginning. . . ."

Anyone probably lives; he is tall, except for a few willows. The forest, the fence, for hundreds. Over and over the fields and the same story.

He said, "yes," transforming everything I've already said. He lives here, in the middle of the lonely poles. The empty rooms came running out; the one-eyed man with a bottle and two glasses. We took our places among them; we drank, bowing deeply.

As soon as I saw his face, his birds, his breath, I was talking; he and I and he compelled us in the very depths of his opened head. Some honeycomb was the evening sky. I spoke tranquilly, stroking black bread; he always agreed with me.

I think neither I nor he has time to wait. I think you know all about the white voice and silver hands. I think other people would be capable of such attention.

That day, the next three days, I can't say how they talked but I listened without constraint, observing idealists, romantics, and other united powers. Eloquence knew submission without conscientious gravity. I had risen far enough and he had seen a lot.

Two or three weeks later, listening to it, the same tricks take place. Turning it in their hands, the pleasure of material goes in search and is completed. He was able to speak with virtual independence, of nothing, of ground and grindstone. He knew where he stood and changed the subject. It completely disappeared.

THE INJURIES

You: who would be avenged: the idea of risk: punish the done wrong. One evening I was wringing his hand, I said, "I have my doubts and I must satisfy them." Hurry with me to my palazzo as soon as my back was turned.

We came cautious down a staircase, stood unsteady on the white ground, gleams with precision up from the damps. "Drink!" I said while that repose was buried around us. His eyes of piled bones into the recesses. It hangs among the moisture at a breath. We continued our route in search of a sign, a flambeau rather than a flame.

At the less spacious end remains a mound. He stepped forward — distant from each other — one had reached, one arrested — "I must leave you in my power" — ejaculated from his astonishment.

At these words have spoken, throwing them aside, with these materials I discovered a long moaning cry — the more satisfaction — or screams from the chained form, the figure within the solid fabric of my midnight hand. I struggled with its weight, its destined position upon my head.

The noise sat down and subsided. A new voice said, "Let it fall."

The most homely narrative would be its own evidence. And today do I dream my soul, but tomorrow, the world. . . .

I spent most of my time with my growth, and in my manhood derived principal pleasure — the nature of the intensity is fidelity. I married a domestic monkey, large, beautiful, and entirely ancient. Our friendship offered personal violence, neglected affection, ill temper. My original soul thrilled my frame, opened it — I slept off the night's debauch, drowned in the excess of memory.

My old heart had once loved me; then came perverseness. One morning it had loved me about its neck, tears streaming no offense. On the night of the day I was aroused from myself, swallowed up, made our escape, resigned to an imperfect chain of facts, examining the words "head" and "bed."

I remembered a garden of fire into my chamber. The walls compressed my spirit into a sentiment of cruelty, into a species of black object on the head, a large hair splotch of the breast; touching it arose against my hand; it would crouch upon my knees, rubbed with caresses.

I had dared the image to work out for me the hot breath of the thing. By day or night I could not remove it from the house. Propped in that position — sand and hair — it couldn't be distinguished from the old anger — imagine the deep blissful detested premises! My heart had beat in innocence, a muscle unexplored; my arms too strong to be restrained. I held in my hands the hideous blessing, swelling with extended sympathy. The dreaded representation was accomplished.

One will take a model for them and become plastically concrete. The conversation sees the words when they want to. Those walks or this figure will come out of most things, but that doesn't mean it's natural. There's a head — how beautiful it is! — if I may call it so. As for me who has eyes it's doubly stimulating, because I'm sitting here in silence — and then to swallow oneself as one is in order to sit down and rest . . . !

A phase of life isn't over then, but one begins more clearly. I feel a power of color, and wonder how it will develop. The clouds of the grass, for instance, when I look at them — that isn't called correctness, or the patches of raining road he felt by a person — himself evidently — while now we can talk it over also suffered in the story. Such calculations don't intend emotion or difficulties; everything is simplified in so far as it's not chaos.

When I say I have my everyday life, everyone must decide for himself. If things had happened the mere suggestion of the thing would occupy a certain rank in my own people. A simple word remains a wound and cannot be healed the first day. I hope you understand what battle this was.

So it is here, inside that evening sky, dark as a cave, most realistically. In order to give you an idea of the shape of a leg they stand in the gardens; on many faces they look faded from nearby, very faded. Narrower strips of color imagine the horizon. The sky covered the sky.

That same spot, if one works, becomes light. What I wanted to say is that we could walk here together.

AT THE HOUR

It happened around the season of cold meat and brandy, with just a hint of gray from the south. Her eyes stranded motorists, vacant like newfound fruit. They do exist, so tenderly, and poured hot tea for the road.

Everyone for a moment tired of us. I'm going to remember without ever knowing it again: this warm silence, this stifled flame in front of the headlights. She glowed far from the central light, awakened against the armrest.

She was talking in a steady grip, motionless. Her breathing had become the hidden embrace. She was staring like the fire, blinked her eyes; attentive to everything that might please us, and wide-open with solitude.

No one moved, rain crackling the air.

INTERSECTION

The man that said the man that wore a purple suit walked soundlessly. The cracked sidewalk flashed with a thin last night. He glanced at the seven-fifteen clock; shadows stood up and stretched in front of his toes. Into the neck of the bottle his face made a smooth huskiness. The street stared without wheels, pressed against a wall.

The thing that had been nothing on the inner edge of the sidewalk. Growling words away from him didn't pause, steps glowed, were gone. Darkness wrapped in dark material, and a dark window above it. His eyes blinked. He listened far off around him.

They don't take prisoners where I'm talking and he won't tell us anything. Blocks where restaurants and drugstores tightened again. A man stood there smoking watching a long drink. The house came along with his eyes until a pair of thick curtains stepped back, and the narrow red carpet and the chipped decanter and the hot ceiling light set hard. Above him grew enormous in the middle of it. The big man bent down awhile, and rubbed his hands together.

In his throat a door at the back was shut. With his mouth open, he held his palm out flat and sent it sailing.

Circumstances — because it was not his name — now life at mine. Being a person — as far as the collection would allow — he pursued these researches within his reach — who was history and relics — in place of the more frequented road. He approached an enormous stone building.

These trees had been watching for him, informed him — being open — he entered, perceived its decorations. Everyone saluted him as they went — his long hand as 'father' — in terms of affection of their attitude which centuries have produced. That a man should cleave unto his friends, oh yes — and in a strange place — an old story — revives unfulfilled hopes and made a beginning. Unlocking this door an observer could see another door.

Raw materials had departed. Soon he found the subject had not been exaggerated — seeing that he was hieroglyphic — to give an outline of the breath of life — remains is left of all this — to see a system mingle with a people and *work.*

This stone could be used as a seal. On it was a face. The words in front are: "O mouth, be my home."

The air shines like finer places, and he nodded toward the sky — the capacities — on them in summer.

Whose mind and whose ambitions about him, servants or peons. In his room should make room for a more active one. Some record of the curious things near the foot of the bed — such things have forgotten the circumstances — taken from him — that was always clear as glass outside the windows. It seems he stands determined — holding this — for reasons.

THE WHEEL

I.

We took something. For ourselves, first, which is the furthest place. In this land with these people I'm only a poor sailor. A point of light upon the surface had happened.

If it should come ride it out — pierced ahead of us the water past her sides like oil — a wall of surface flying. In the glare experience strained and rocked, we were boiling down a gutter, heads to burst, and to them the large body paralyzed as it fell. Afterwards, every detail was staring them in the face.

There, rested — the vanished — gasping but unharmed. Such moonlight beat down the seas, filled us with that talisman, the sky. This is our existence, in which the present seemed to fade. Beneath the wind — drawn skin begin to warming — we stood when what had happened in his lifted hands — holding out his hand — its owner: himself and his companions. The place has a name in that neighborhood: We-Are-Missing.

Then we rose, having no choice, for our own air was leading the way. A map of the world formed new shapes, grew thin, and opened in its center; so high we were — it at our feet — the valley filled with streams, reeds, oak. Here it will be different. Here there is every action whitening in that forest, chance. Here lay down the rod of power, weighed down by the memories.

We descended with their purple pods and reaping hooks; their monotonous faces were standing in person — pull to pieces resemblance — composing each other. Chocolate — the night — was served to us in silver cups — the moon — while the whistling wings — the lake — lapping shone the luminous walls — the city — so far to reach. Our eyes took possession of our feet.

No sound, and the silence calling the hours. This night the wide gates come home again. You, in the wilderness, swept by the waterway. Look at me: through an open doorway: home again.

Because of the lightness, let him go. You should sing as I do, brought in at the door. Of this I am certain: we shall be drawn into it.

Forward, my great purposes

II.

Ripples spread and from them rose two arms towards the bed; a soft deep voice — pearls — the thread. Displaying his eyes, his teeth, her big shoulder. Blue wandering curtain, she lay around the neck of her disorder. The sun overdecorated the room.

She pinned her remembrance on two doors, thud of a foot, and talcum powder. Bits and pieces sticking to mirrors to meet his bluish gaze. She saw him — he saw her — open the gates — one leg and shook her head: "Nothing lasts forever out of the house."

Everything in the room — their stalks — in massive wood from the young arid road — have I come this way? — completely surrounded — coming to life in the depth of a chair — his involuntary gesture, physical presence.

"I remember," she said, "her little arms in the air, subjugation of Sunday afternoon, the past tense of a brandy glass. As a boy his kitchen lisp — milky immersions — cat licks, a little masterpiece of ablution . . ." trailing along the passages. He pirouetted while she jotted down calculations on his tongue. He was tucked away in that cubbyhole, a past made up of a cream sauce with me —

merely friends — this place risen at each other, his rolling breath and her larger fingers. She held his breath like someone listening. Frothy moonlight — she began touching it everywhere — the night pours what they were thinking to the limit.

III.

I'm sitting here — the failure of things — as one is — all this complicated material must be beautiful. To speak about the white heat of iron — it seems cold — wrapped in a firm hand of nature — words also white-hot. I was finding more that isn't perfect, and feel older in order to ripen.

I'm sentimentalism — and the harvest isn't here. I'm a phase of life toward the opinion of the world — better tear up this letter as well. A black coat with a greasy collar and the cycle of seasons. This morning, haze was style and character in the dunes. An impression came into my head which I intend to spend.

I feel grateful for practical things in good shape: pew, checkered dress, an old brush. In a drugstore I found a basket — more detail is possible.

A kneeling figure of a man, of a woman gathering the expression "I hope you don't think of my tired brains in questions of right and wrong." I'm at work, I take him on my lap, the bad turn out well.

I'm simple to fall back on the whiteness of a white-washed wall, and go and stand in the fields showing a wet man on a muddy road — the sentiment is a silhouette — a few tree trunks, concentrating on the wood.

I had a baby, afterwards a mother, like a lily among thorns. In the evening the lighted mud puddles look cozy from my window.

What expanse, what calmness, between me and the ordinary world — a permanent address — with the fixed idea of potatoes — deeper obstacles — and grasp my petition for membership, interior with the blue of cloth and another blue of doubt.

I get thick lips in a big size of the broken indigo and secret bronze. Summer is a low roof, winter is walking violet. The best thing I know is the difference between you and me, and the technique improves every year.

IV.

The house wobbled — illusion in the sun — it was pale black — a gull suspended — exhibiting obscurely from all body going out into the world.

It — with the other — which was loose — explosion in the depths, wind-swept unpolluted piece of bone. A great experiment is such a handful, and the wind rising. It lit up on the table white cotton and brown wool, water streaming down the windows, who was bending over a lamp long ago, with the gold line around it, and upon the hills which trembled in its fury, jerking the waves.

The little boys under the sheet — half-opened eyes — turning sulfurous until a white shape bulged out. Triangular letters — each line going down the table — drugged the iron pillars of the pier. It changes — amplifies — the turnpike, the faded ticket, the leaves in her hand.

Like an eye upon the bed it stood open, dropped by a hawk. A woman came back — everything she did — and asked the time — green dust on the horizon — him coming to a more distant ridge — hidden beneath her cloak — it come tumbling in the armchair, reflected full in the face in her eyes, settling deeper.

White drops from the blade, swimming green in the ripples, shifted an edge in the water and the sky shifted. His hand praised the column, the gate, the sky. It isn't simple, or pure; one calls it — corridors of brain — gripping the arm of the chair — as if, in his place, a city would be burning there, behind the balanced walls, fierce on the staircase.

The people stood and let them in. They have no houses. The streets are each other. Beneath the pavement it conveyed things, buy things, passing a hand into the complexity of box after box — between the stalls and tasted the sweetness of labyrinth — suspended above their heads the observer choked with observations.

This box — lying back in his chair — lacked self-consciousness. Surveying it — flourishing in obscurity, distorted — suggesting thick shirts, stiff sheets, swollen violin. The street in deep folds — wrap themselves in every shop — beneath the hissing gas as the afternoon wore on.

White discs through ivory pages, sleek in the rain. Seeking some landing — rolling energy — into the flocks of small birds, brushing the grass. It swells the tulips in this dusk and sat speechless under the electric light. A far away humming was her stooping heart, answering the little boys, high in mid air.

Foam would shine through us, an aspiration of this cradling. It lay on her lap, feasting on scarlet, flourishing his wine glass across the table. Here is a scrap in the puckered morning, pressing both hands into drifting sunlight. It was a country shuffling along strange roads on your own — stuck to them, the eyes of a foreigner — floating in the body immersed in things, falling into thin sheets, fertility.

Everything remained — it as an inheritance — shaped against trees in white hollows one blazing afternoon. Of force rushing in patterns — first one foot, then the other — vapors thickened where the cadaverous streets and the dust itself thick were spattered particles circling deeper. It bent slightly as they reached it. It stirs the curtains, swaying between strokes, imprinting faces.

V.

You watched the flickering on the ceiling — smooth skin — when you opened the door through the shadows — a great actor preparing to leave — the ocean was set boiling again from your astonished body — the traces there — listening, raising the sky to your level.

The great city above the houses was reliving twilights, gone down from night to day, day to nights. Your voice on your mouth — our separation — I want your dry bones — bread and time — looking into it from very close — unheard on a map, green or black, no one has seeded.

Against a pink cushion melting and dissolving — drinking from you as a commonplace conception — your hermaphrodite vanity — spangled with the rain — nails grow longer, a springtime plant — belching constellations from their vessels, and use them to cover the walls of my hut. One day at the seashore I was inside your skin. Flattened before taking a single step.

Still, as you are, not in the foreground, nearer the sacrifices, walking at random — two travelers, our childhood — decomposed in my stained fingertips — each shovel-full as it fell — to hold back the soldiers when we want to photograph — at the gates with palms on the horizon like a train, an immensity.

A proliferation of houses made of rushes, windows on the water — I thought my tongue was on fire — swinging back into place after the wind has stopped. Initiators have breathed into your mouth, inserting tongues in beautiful poses — translations — excited by the great monuments and droppings of birds. You rubbed your stomach against them; they put it in their boats and returned home.

They call after you, rolling like wheels. I walked through those streets and walked through them again. I went away and have remained so. You have been superimposed on the lower part of this body, drawn back and tied together. The pink sun undressed over your eyes.

You lay down on branches, a lamp hanging on the wall. The night stayed long and came back — many other ferocious sweet things — you never ceased to be present — the idea of the subject — motionless, covered with powder, an arm around each other.

VI.

They made shovels with their inch-long fingernails by its inhabitants of that name.

A man, stripped to the waist, spread night soil. Girls on the flat rocks at the edge of the public road.

Peel and pare their part — passed through his hands — until the big full kernels under pressure had nowhere to run. They fashioned parallels through the doorless aperture that was the only entrance to their home.

They looked up, plunged into the room over and over again. Within reach of their hands — coming for me — in which we have been taught to shiver — to grasp the change before a new pattern could be created.

They came over the hill laughing — in sunlit corners of the backbone all sewn in. The heat was intense — luxuriantly — scouring the hills for ashes — anything organic — stimulated to the collection point.

They watched the sky encircle us — that enlargement — remolding each other. Across that distance we leaned all afternoon. . . .

It was impossible for me to move from one foot to the other. I can hardly remember to close my trousers here. What the town is like, what walks it has. I want to be one of those bootlickers who have abused their positions. I'm filled with indignation at description. There was a great uprising.

Only one man has my love — he'll receive my indifference and scorn! — and that same man — into your eyes burn for him — I think only of these confessions, you are no longer a woman I desire. I have lost sincerity, forced to yield these explanations, wandering around your banal arms, your contradictory eyes, speed breath, object being, cult.

There are — I beg you — scribbled messages: let me throw myself at your word you have chosen among all men — so desirable in your talent. What?! You won't say it! I'll wait (in a completely disinterested way) and refuse the diseased mistrust you send me!

I need a lot of money. I can see it will appear *mad to you.* To live with a person who shows no gratitude as her property against the side table in the very place of repose is not moral intelligence, though flirtation was even greater than my grief. I'll tell you another time about the political events and the overwhelming influence they exerted on me.

He who wrote these lines in deepest humility is their theme. I'd feel I was failing in my duty to obey private language if I didn't tell you whose talents arouse my sympathy all his mad adventures. I merely added the word pantheism in a *new sense.* The melancholy truth is full of reproaches. Persecute me.

He laughed — any objection? — I said something behind me without being invited — and crossed his legs under a hundred million bucks pushed out — big power — and looked at the big brown freckles around his eyes. His desk sees you down at the water — unless you were in it. I stood up — the smear — yanked open a shadow on the wall — a guy is anybody but himself — facing a blank slit in his armored face.

The meatgrinder goes back to work. Something is missing that makes all the difference. A handkerchief wiped his lips and his fingers where the presence of a witness said nothing of his silence. To him I was a trophy. I would be ashamed of that. I'm ashamed of nothing.

He got home in about an hour — it shook him — into the shower with the whole thing dumped in the reservoir. He shot a hole in his ceiling. It was a sigh of relief.

Came back alone, sat down, and waited. Me, I understand cold skin — I like everybody — I've got work to do — whom you have heard called a clear space — by making it black on white — this morning, a straight reproduction from the original.

AFTER

The moon of darkness came, mounted the bed — aimless lamentation — where trees in the light labor — littered pieces — shooting the human shape on the opposite wall, bedroom floor.

Of the wind, of the reiterating sea: hooting of birds. Under the bed some channel mumble out old song.

A leaf stirring the pool turned to uneasy stars, turn some alien crystal hard in the passing rain — yellow streamer — in the lull of ominous summer bounty — pelting serenity.

One on top of another the plants were standing there. And the dusted flowers full of ribbon — all the attics — burst with giant grass — sinking have turned on the ruined boards — clasped their cramped rows, swollen, closing over them.

It might be changed.

An insect on the pillow in the open room. The beauty of the clean still bed flowing down his eyes. The dark folds — breaking in measure — evenly.

FORWARD OR BACK

Its eyes falling back against the interior of their cylinders, opened — thus laying — both their embarrassments, his dress, his extremity. A fabulous reconstitution of fear — she lit a cigarette — does something to a person's identity — hands trembled — into the head as a spoon of thought of the night — velvet piss — of one city for me while I'm coming to seek the world.

Into the testimony of the two — of the other — from the waist with the back eye in a dark place — contraction — full of permission to touch itself upon your rumpled chest of hair, a sediment.

He get crime. Drags upward while the thin flesh — it means fury — it is in her — inhaling among the debris pushed into the pillow. A different rage: the egg portion of night. His partners pound the horizontal muscles of a man's beloved.

The estrangement is on the neck of the creature, husked. I'm coming to know a detachment with one hand — sitting between twilights — by the girl I am I may be those circular years — the face of uncertainty from which love and fear are shining — it loves one of them — muted, holding her hands through the target, in the toilets without aim, kneeling between tongues.

The waters make you immortal. The song — its other name — is "Eyes Wide Open." There is no direct way. Distinction radiating.

She has the face of the subject, the feeling of removal, orifices of someone else, and is collecting the rest of destiny. Have been born by degrees to the narrative who was leaning forward.

We have a restless place awaiting you — this particular night with a knowledge mixed eye to eye — they come eternally into it alone — rummaging through photographs who had been spared a face but twined with ivy. I saw her pouring down the steps — dropping the cloak of his neck — shoulders sideways like a cat — kissed upon their knees my health and put it in words, throne for the deed.

I want a thing in the world full of minor objects thicker than contemplation. Thick ones with their sweet collected creation. He went a long way beyond what they are to himself. Sitting there shaking at opposite ends with connections.

One had forces marching in silence — the most venomous kind — without intermission, smashed like a bitter plate — Napoleonic colonels had made their title clear. Something begins — frozen hard — even a mattress — with the men — such as it is — helpless on the field, the city worse — have burst from the wounds a telegraphic message to get well.

Right through the bladder and coming back out — Washington waters with all its features — entering us like a wedge — through the helpless foliage, flashes of fire, crashing men, groans in an open space with the fresh smell of blood blown off the face or head — amid the woods, masses; mortal purposes up there, a few stars.

Is sleeping soundly at this moment, a hole straight through the lungs. He lies naked — the stimulants of every object bleached from his cheeks — the strangeness of perfect hair, green eyes — hold onto my hand — ashy apple — shot in the head with a few words, wants nothing, emanating artillery and slow blows of axes. Some piles of men — thick pontoons — dripping their handsome faces, superfluous flesh.

You desire him. There hangs something. His absence.

The space near it looked like the sky, specimens of unworldliness. . . .

The men may have been odd, but they fell before me like a murmur. Each has its peculiarities with blank paper — doctrine, confession, recitation; the problem is to organize principles out of it; in the present struggle: tender waste.

He was among the first fighting. He lived three days, so that the brains lay there in the open air. Their backs were in different parts of their bodies, inscriptions pinned to their breasts. In places you have this opportunity. He died yesterday.

I walked home about sunset. A boy called to me. I stood impassive as my stupid eye just occurred.

Some had blankets around their shoulders — strips and streamers and meat — through the long apartments — former winters — to follow his passionate action in a subtile world of air — a different sunlight, full of whirling rage — long, long before they were due.

Without parallel, down to this hour. There have been samples of another description, but his eyes will never be written.

From the glowing prostration and the marrow of constant rain.

AT THE FOOT OF THE STAIRS

B lives in the country with a constant companion: inside arrows. The arrow is chasing women — enchantress! — so B can be the most beautiful and useless. Take her away from senseless existence or leave her alone!

Jewels burst with envy; what about you? There was a foggy full moon thickening through a storm — before her, behind her — no one sees, she enters with white curtains — flowers of her action — threshold where the clock wound into her hair — you must lie, "Everything here used to be ugliness, but my heart is kind."

"I am a monster but hide it with wit. I am a castle but horror walks along the wall. Water surrounded by dogs. Hands wearing a dark velvet dress."

The clock was awaiting you — stand up, father — taking orders outside the door — burning a troubled look on her face, watching every single morning, remember your promise. She'd rather lie on the sheets with full sleeves and translucent exhibition. Dress me, arrange my hair; she embraces herself onto the bed in despair and listens.

Her message breaks her promises. "I've forgotten the magic words." It's something like *fabulous clothes for madame* or *mysteriously left at the door for you* or *climb up after me.*

She looks away, a target fixed on the wall. The floor comes up — as they do — shining like clouds.

IN THE FLESH

I.

Billy giving them just enough light — naked on a bench inflated — he's got sleepless night — dancing in his mind showering waiting for glimpses — it's so big down here. "Relax," Coach said like melting, some spit from one corner of his mouth — through the window as the freshman — "keep your voice from getting carried away while we're still schoolboys."

As he combed his hair — the comb through his hair — glassy eyes rubbing — the look in his eyes splashing. . . .

Billy — pink — his pink towel — pink legs outstretched — split open and force his mouth — from his rural home to the highway rest-stop, drink. His most serious dad — suspect what he was doing — trembled in the stomach — Billy running down white porcelain, photographing. "What're you doing in there?" "I think I gotta shit."

In the leather easy chair — autumn on the backyard — shapes created by a fire — on the thick carpeting, "Dad?" — hesitation — "Do I have to go with all those other guys in the woods?" The kid was changing, because the kid looked worshipful — when he didn't have to — gazed at his barefooted — small, on the other hand, defined — sometimes gruff with the boy — trying to calm his breathing had shook him up — his own or the boy's? —

whose renegade twinge some late evening has been rebuilt in each bedroom, larger than kingsize.

Out of the corner of his eye Billy was looking, Billy could smell — it was himself from where he stood, his own in response — had to quickly found himself — get a move on — with his own definite tension restlessly in their denser secluded faces. . . .

As if he'd been hit with a cream pie — up in the air down his throat — I wanna believe the words — an explosion in the sunny spot — aimed at a human being this time as if seeing him for the first time — letting himself be another boy, the two boys, some kind of son doing down there — unable to say the words off his forehead — loud in the still air.

Billy gasped, nearly purple — holding hands for support — glanced at each other — they both fell several times — searched frantically for the moment and began to lick the wounds. His back, his front, his body out long — what I am doing would never recover — just acting, not thinking — pressed into one smooth motion rolled back his life. No man had ever — his father's mouth — never enough tongue — turned back into his blue eyes, wider than before. His lips shuddered throughout his body. "Billy" — into Billy — he clung to the man — "How does it feel to be a mouth?"

II.

An entire summer with my dead mother's brother's sons: I could hardly wait! They go to church in the fields; I want to be in there with them. I flexed, I soaped — corn silk — I would unfold each new adventure of each new day. My cousins' suntans.

I shook hands with all-knowing uncle — corn on the cob, blackberry cobbler — unpack — they watched me — wanting and doing his scattered brown hair down your spine. I remembered summers sleeping — that praise — in the stable with the horses and the milking machine.

Atop the clean white sheets watching each other — length and size — sleep tight in the breeze each form breathing to claim our veins, channels . . . "Are you asleep yet?" "I can't sleep."

I like that.

We traded kisses to experiment heartbeats. His body flew to my mouth — he was trying to keep from screaming — exploding the snowy sheets in the dark nests of his sweetness — he — doing as I had done — pulling his breath into his knees in a rush of white.

"Is that the lesson for today?"
"No, this is . . ."

III.

Jimmy was cute; he buried his face in socks. He picked up one of the school jerseys and gazed at the sight of himself. He lifted wet fingers and achieved sensations. Watching himself he was watching himself.

A guy wearing a guy over his nose — sweaty eggs — he inhaled peppery flanks, wiggled his toes. He swayed — streaming thought in the world — drunk against his unbelievable fingers — superman rain — strained to hold himself still. Football practice was finished.

Hal stood facing him, gym bag in hand. You know how it is: a man lays down.

"I won't say a word" — don't say another word — he studied, stepped back, didn't move, sit up, got up, started to, go ahead, I guess so, I hope so, turned toward Jimmy, the distant and romantic past.

He leaned down his soft legs — sheen of shower soap — beads of a necklace — down on your animal hands and knees — shiver through conflicting orders — thrilled at being a clear pearl — planted on the floor.

Jimmy watched Hal leaned over, tangled his eyes, jockey briefs on the door knob, of his neck pulling slowly by the hair up toward — and turned every muscle in his body to perfumed oil, filling the air.

The long lines of his high back closed around his hips. His nipples were bubbling under the cobra heart. Radiation all over the floor. He could actually hear energy — scalp sizzled — their breaths slumped over them, expressionless.

Absent-minded sweaty face. He looked down at himself. Now I finish my shower. Now I see your face again. Now I leave this place — whirled — waiting for the sounds of Hal's leaving — distant sound of the locker room door. Now I can't sit down.

Cove high school at the top of the blossoming hill. The sky stood looking — making it autumn — late afternoon — a state of euphoria in the laundry room — watching them in silence — hovered and flushed with heat — from the row of lockers after school had closed. Jimmy in the air — waiting for something — I'm one of you — another knot in his throat.

IV.

He could do it. It's all right. Jason in his arms. "Thanks, Dad, but I'm all right." At arm's length — "I care a lot" — unbuttoned his shirt — "I'll show you" — pulled off his socks — "how much I" — hugged together — "care."

"You, too!" He could hardly stand up — buried his nose in disbelief, disappeared into his son's mouth.

Jason was panting — my skin — the boy — my Dad — out of him — inside his body. Rhythmically deeper — perfectly vertical inside — to the level of both their heads — Jason's room lit by the streetlight, hunkered down in the moonlight, pouring his lips over another world, distant, deep, content.

He felt such terror against the side of the mattress. The boy lay before him, wrapped with relief. He was doing a darn good job of acting. He lowered over his sleeping son.

The boy in the mirror, his thick eyes from under his eyebrows — a tranquilizer — all the years — "How do I look?" — milking a smile, making him drunk. . . .

Jason gasped, repeating that thought in his mind. He felt as big as inside him — the popping wind — looking back into his brain — farther backward — had turned to flame around the edges of the cool air. He pushed with them, rubbed against the same person. The room in slow motion — he couldn't stop smiling — you and me — flapped through his body — could hardly hold it — you — enormous — again and again and again tonight.

We watch the sun come up; then watch it fall in the slippery air. . . .

Thoughts went through his mind. He wondered if they could read his mind.

Dad could conjure up the next room. Home with his hand raised in victory — all the guys swarmed around him — the team — buddies from way back — I'm the son of a coincidence — because this evening, if you pinched yourself, you were awake and dreaming, his voice echo from neck to toes to go all the way.

From just saying his name hot water ran in sheets across the floor.

AGAINST THE WINDOWS

The faces under the rays coated with liquid — obsess the taut eyes — sleek cheeks, star on the forehead in the place where fixity has started — and arches his astonishing back.

The crowd against each other seems to spring from the building in the thunder of clapping, carried around on shoulders.

A woman improvises with her arms, dances an inward peel with precision. Against the windows — flushed homage — bare neck in little sips — someone is letting go — gust of air — sloping stairs under the faded curtain — settling in a powder. . . .

They're waving their hands the way they grow smaller. A seed ceases to be held.

Beneath us it can be read like a picture, motionless.

He traveled, cut his works, ordered foundation. One part is the city, one part read it aloud. He knocks — pattern of strength — forcing him anywhere, restored to called by name.

When he called, the image of time washed her hands and threw it into the wilderness. His face entered a long road — there's a man shooting over the hills — he set his face in the direction of traps and pits. Animals fled from his body. I, who changes fates, belong where people are everyday — yourself an enemy — you in dreams — the skilled people massed over the city — compared with everything in the house of incantation.

He went up — wraps up his hair — the steps on the roof up her restless sleep — push him to go — until the day he has removed evil. Now I adopt you. Throw away month or year, now I will carry his body back to us.

Brought to silence — the mountain lifts its tree — they dug a pit, the wind brought a dream. *You didn't touch me. His filthy clothes roared. He put on his crown — horns of amber — a mauve back door turned him into the garden where the dead renumber the living. He shaped his mouth to speak, your name fell into it.*

They withdrew they sat down they washed their walk-along hands. Being collected — the road into your house

— your resting dwelling place — in a great bed embraces his treasure for you — if one takes it one lives there — filling glasses with water where I entered — and reads aloud to her.

Like an eagle I circled over him. Like a goldsmith he fashioned an image of your body.

WORLD

That day reality — and by no man of earth — was going out to be hunted. At moonset — his chief seat — he woke there. He couldn't see anything.

This forest is thick; that must be why several women evoking pleasant images soon faded. She followed it; the quarry must have changed its course. He stopped. This place can't be a right place. Before his eyes bodies colder than snow leapt over him.

It was moving, it was coming — wish it was something else — of a wind at the stranger unbidden — what is it? — glint of carcass in the deep voice — our world is one — he understood — forced upon him in which all things took shape, form after form among us because we make room. He looked hard at the trees — they burned through his skull — "Tell me what to do and I will do it."

Shape will be on you, neither a man nor my queen — he has arts — he looked down and saw hands shaped like hands. A heaving might have torn loose the warm young flesh he was used to. I will have his things — walking away from yourself — and he will have mine.

The musicians were keeping time as if they were being made by one Thing.

He saw it, but he was too late. When they found him, a great black scale fell to the earth.

They were in a wood of her tales. She sat whittling leaves. The wind glittered like foam. It seemed real.

A great bird descends from the sky.
Its beak gleamed in the red light.
Through them poured the cool breeze.
The birds have dreamed me beneath the apple trees.

IN THE MIST

On Monday the window was open; the night followed me and couldn't be quieted. I smoked at the sky, lay down in the rain — blind devotion — for a person mirrored in the sea the sky is melodic.

He was a man — (fear the awakening) — a woman — (my lovers passed in illusion) — I rode in a forest — (religious instinct?) — opened the exaggerated sun — a kind of sweating lassitude.

I lie on my couch — everything has changed — patience of the mists — pump into the entrails of things — he sucks up sunlight, pounding with joy, precise as a cello. Someone comes along and separates me from the form. Evangelical milk and humanitarian thighs and socialist drapery. It's not enough to have wings; when I unfold them your perfume rises from the paper.

Great stretches of water — a gray vapor that appears to be moving — sunset melted dark ink — mass of trees — my ministerial partition — with the space of days before an address. As dancers ripple and retreat their faces remain movements of a body.

I thought of her dance without meaning, whistling through the bushes. My feet ahead of me — one among others — trembling resources — between that enormity and the moon on the hilltop here. Now I can hear part of myself penetrated by individualities. The city is immense.

This changeable sky sees the buildings differently. There are more flowers in the house than in the ground. The floor a forest of dark olive trees, sea at the far end. . . .

Shadows glide beyond the plains with white sails — almost in the air — moving noiselessly over the surface of things. Another ocean climbed the mist, adjusting that human anatomy: horizon lines. I forget what I stayed at home to do. The blue spread out.

With my elbows on the table I'm going back to that place.

Author's Note:

As collage, *Into Distances* derives language from the writings of Djuna Barnes, Charles Baudelaire, Franklin Brooks, Raymond Chandler, Jean Cocteau, Colette, Thad Fargo, Gustave Flaubert, Jean Genet, The Gilgamesh Poet, H. Rider Haggard, Nathaniel Hawthorne, William Hinton, James Joyce, Kevin Killian, Edgar Allan Poe, Sarah Schulman, Agnes Smedley, Ivan Turgenev, Vincent Van Gogh, Evangeline Walton, Walt Whitman, and Virginia Woolf.

NEW AMERICAN POETRY SERIES (NAP)

1. *Fair Realism*, Barbara Guest
2. *Some Observations of a Stranger at Zuni in the Latter Part of the Century*, Clarence Major
3. *A World*, Dennis Phillips
4. *A Shelf in Woop's Clothing*, Mac Wellman
5. *Sound As Thought*, Clark Coolidge
6. *By Ear*, Gloria Frym
7. *Necromance*, Rae Armantrout
8. *Loop*, John Taggart
9. *Our Nuclear Heritage*, James Sherry
10. *Arena*, Dennis Phillips
11. *I Don't Have Any Paper So Shut Up*, Bruce Andrews
12. *Gematria*, Jerome Rothenberg
13. *Into Distances*, Aaron Shurin

For a complete list of our poetry publications
write us at Sun & Moon Press
6026 Wilshire Boulevard
Los Angeles, California 90036